Maria's Wish

Once upon a time, there lived a girl named Maria, she was charming.

Everyone in Webster town loved her.

She always had a big smile on her face and was always ready to help.

Everyone, even at school, Maria was well known for her kindness.

She always wanted to make everyone feel better.

She was quick to offer assistance when needed.

She was happy when others around her were happy; no one passed by Maria without smiling.

Even if they were sad once they saw her.

Her warm smile was enough to make them feel better.

Although Maria was pretty and kind.

She couldn't sing as well as her two best friends, Louisa, and Shelley, who were very good singers.

They had beautiful voices, and Maria admired that about them.

Whenever Louisa and Shelley sang, Maria was sad because she could not sing.

She wasn't jealous, she was just sad.

Because she loved music but didn't have the voice to sing beautifully.

"If only I could sing as beautifully as Louisa and Shelley.

If only I didn't have this croaky voice," Maria would whine miserably.

Since Maria couldn't sing, her friends didn't ask her to join their band; they felt that she would only ruin their beautiful songs with her croaky voice.

Although Maria tried her best not to show it.

She was upset because of it, she felt left out whenever they talked about their music and didn't tell her about it.

The two friends often would talk about music.

New songs, the band, and much other music-related stuff and not carry Maria along.

They felt it was unnecessary to discuss music with her because she couldn't sing.

This made Maria very sad most times.

Each time they began to talk about music, Maria's heart ached.

I wish I could sing; Maria would always say to herself when no one was listening.

She was good at hiding how sad she felt, and no one noticed.

Her friends didn't know that she was sad.

She felt left out when they spoke about music or sang.

Every day, Maria practiced several times in the shower.

No matter how hard she tried to sing, her voice never came out right.

"If only I could sing half as good as Louisa and Shelley.

Then I wouldn't feel so miserable.

If I can't sing, then what's so special about me?" Maria would ask herself.

As time went on, Maria got so distressed that she couldn't sing, and soon she couldn't hide how sad and left out she felt.

The people in town began to notice that Maria was no longer her happy self.

She no longer stopped to help the traders in the market or dropping some money for the beggars.

Even at school, Maria was no longer
her usual self.

She always wore a long frown on her
face and hardly paid attention during
class.

"Maria, what's the matter with you,
you hardly smile anymore.

Your face is always sad and gloomy,"
many would ask.

Maria didn't tell anyone what the problem was.

I think I should sleep more.

She would say and avoid saying what made her feel sad.

One cool evening, Maria was out on the terrace, clutching her pink teddy bear to her chest.

Louisa and Shelley had organized a concert in school.

They hadn't even told her about it.

As she had watched them sing, putting on matching outfits and the whole school cheering them in a frenzy.

She didn't know when tears started rolling down her cheeks.

They're supposed to be my best friend.

They should have told me about their plans even if I couldn't sing.

They could have gotten me the same outfit if we were friends.

Many thoughts ran through her mind.

As she gazed up at the sky, she suddenly saw a shooting star.

Maria was quick to make a wish "I wish to sing as good as Louisa and Shelley" Maria wished.

As quickly as Maria made her wish.

She suddenly realized that her voice
was no longer croaky and hoarse.

She could now sing beautifully.

"Now I can be so happy," Maria said
joyfully.

"The world will hear my voice.

Louisa and Shelley will plead with me to join their band.

I'm now special; Maria danced happily and wiped her tears.

However, the happiness didn't last.

At first, when she sang, it surprised everyone.

Even her two friends were surprised.

"Maria, please join our band; we had no idea you could sing so well, they said.

For a month, Maria and her friends organized several concerts, she thought she was having the best time of her young life. She was no longer sad and didn't feel left out.

No one complained that she didn't help them or look cheerful.

However, after a while Maria realized that she still felt empty.

She could only sing as well as Louisa and Shelley; she couldn't sing better than them.

Soon, Maria was no longer satisfied.

She wished she could sing better than Louisa and Shelley.

If I could just sing better than them.

Perhaps it would make me happy and satisfied, and this emptiness would go away, Maria said.

She kept having many thoughts on how to sing better and be better.

She was so deep in thoughts that she looked sad and lost.

She was still having these thoughts, when a farmer passing by asked her why she looked so sad.

Maria told the farmer about her wish and how she didn't feel happy.

Even though she could sing as well as her friends.

I wish I could sing better than them, she told him.

The farmer sighed long and hard before giving her a piece of advice that stayed in her heart forever.

"Dear Maria, happiness doesn't lie in the things we can do.

I'm afraid that even if you can sing better than your friends, you still won't be happy.

Happiness isn't when we have everything, it's when we're happy even when we have nothing.

"Maria pondered on his words as she walked home.

He was right; if she sang better than her friends, she would still want something more.

However, she realized she was happy when she loved herself for who she was before becoming envious of her friends.

Singing better doesn't define who she was.

Maria decided to appreciate herself, not by what she had or admired, but by who she was.

Day by day, she learned to love herself and make others happy.

The more she put a smile on others' faces.

The more she worried less about singing better.

As time went on, she didn't go to more concerts or desire many matching outfits.

She wasn't even bothered when her friends talked about music or a new show.

As she embraced herself for who she was, she felt better.

Looked better, smiled more, and was happy with herself.

She realized that she was unique in her way.

She didn't have to have the best voice, or the coolest dance moves.

She was unique in her way, everyone was unique.

The next time she saw the farmer, she thanked him.

Maria didn't worry if she slept and woke up and she couldn't sing again.

She had discovered who she was and what made her happy.

She wasn't going to trade it for even the coolest voice in the world.

Every time Maria felt less special, she would remember the words of the kind farmer, and she would smile.

Happiness is a choice, and she chose to be happy whether she could sing or not.

THE END